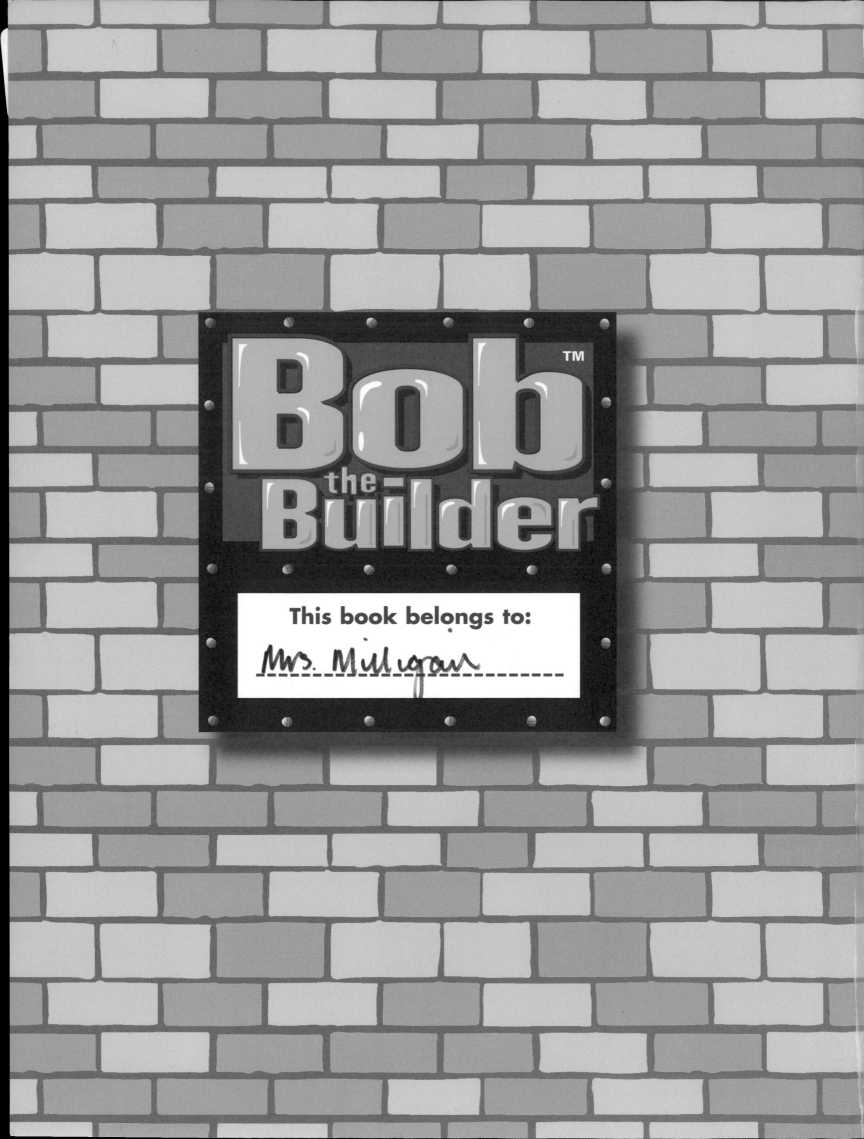

Bob the Builder™

This book belongs to:

Mrs. Milligan

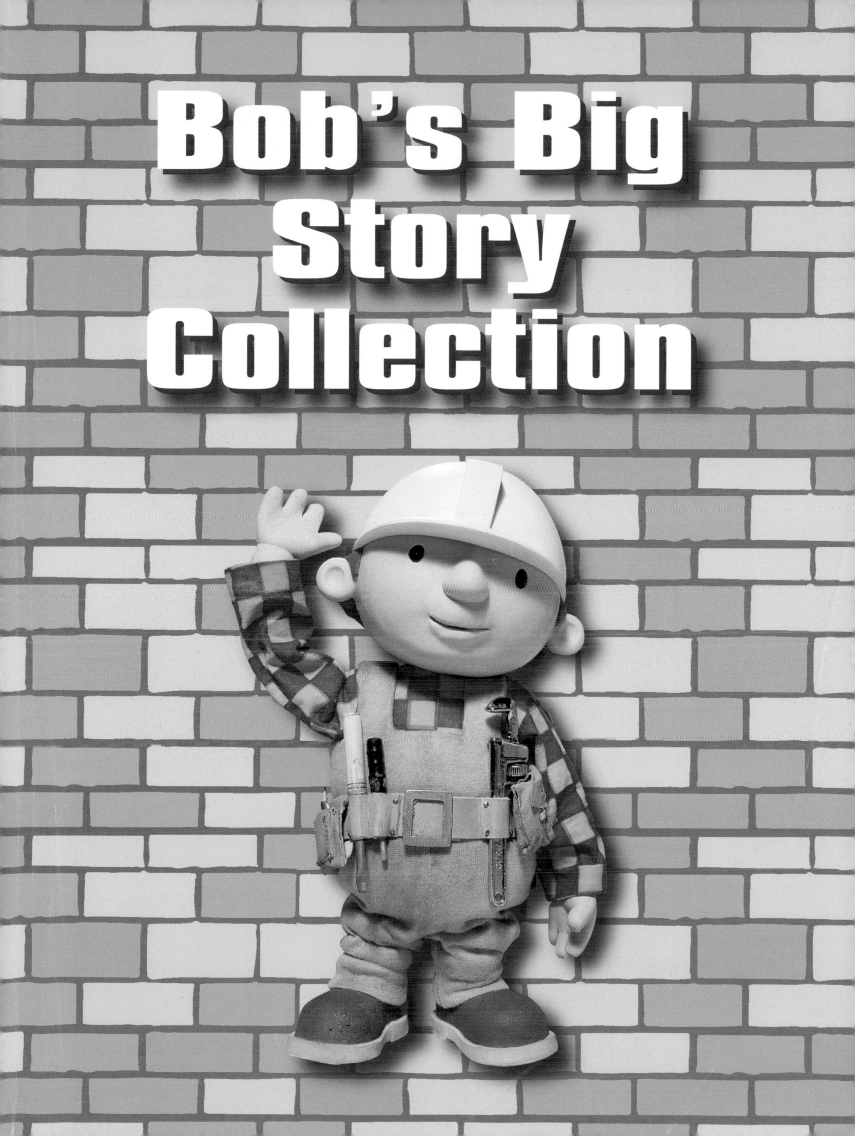

Bob's Big Story Collection

Contents

I hope you enjoy this book. There are two sorts of stories in the collection – the **Short** stories are just right to dip into, and there are **Longer** ones which make perfect bedtime stories!

Can you read it?
Yes, you can!

Pilchard Goes Fishing

Muck and Scoop could hear some very strange noises coming from inside Bob's house.

"Keep still! Honestly!" they heard Bob say.

"I wonder what's going on," said Scoop.

"Morning everyone!" called Wendy as she arrived at the yard. "Where's Bob?"

"He's in the house, but we don't know what he's doing," replied Muck.

"It's no use wriggling like that…" they could hear Bob saying.

Wendy went in to find out what was going on.

"Bob! What are you doing?" asked Wendy.
"I thought it was time that I cleaned out Finn's
tank. Only, he's not helping, are you, Finn?"
said Bob.

"It doesn't look easy," said
Wendy as she watched Bob trying
to catch the goldfish in a little net.
Pilchard watched Bob and Finn
and licked her lips.

"Oh no, look at the time!" said Bob as he put the net down and grabbed his hat.

"Don't worry, you get going. I'll deal with Finn. I'll see you later," Wendy said as Bob dashed out.

"Miaow!" Pilchard said. She was still watching the tank, very carefully.

"Yes, I know, Pilchard," said Wendy, "I'll just sort out a few things in the office, then we'll clean Finn!"

"Miaow!" said Pilchard, very loudly.

Bob rushed out of the house and started to organise the machines.

"Right, come on everyone! We've got lots of different jobs to do today. Muck, I'll need you to help me, and I'll need Dizzy and Roley, too," he said.

"**Can we fix it?**" called Scoop.

"**Yes, we can!**" everyone shouted, as Bob jumped onto Muck's step and they set off.

Bob and the team pulled up in front of the tunnel.

"Shall I start mixing, Bob?" asked Dizzy.

"Yes, Dizzy. You do that… Oh bother! I've forgotten the cement. Muck, would you mind going back to the yard and getting a couple of bags of cement, please?" asked Bob.

"On my way, Bob!" said Muck happily, as he drove off.

"Please hurry! We've got loads to do today!" called Bob after Muck.

9

"Now come on, Finn," tutted Wendy. "That's it!" she said as she scooped him into the net. "I'll just put you somewhere safe," she added as she flopped Finn into a bucket of water.

"Miaow!" said Pilchard, as she watched Wendy.

Just then there was a loud screeching noise out in the yard.

"Ohh, that sounds like Muck," said Wendy as she grabbed the bucket and rushed outside.

10

She was just in time to see Muck swerve to avoid Bird, then skid across the yard and bang into the lean-to. The wooden support broke and fell into Muck's front scoop with a bang. Wendy rushed over.

"Are you all right, Muck?" she asked.

"I'm OK. I'm sorry. Bob sent me back for some cement and he said to hurry, so I did and went a bit fast and… you won't tell Bob will you?" said Muck, speaking very quickly.

"Oh, Muck, Bob would understand," said Wendy.

"Pleeease, Wendy, I feel silly," said Muck.

"OK, I won't tell him," agreed Wendy.

"The lean-to shouldn't be too hard to fix," said Wendy.

"Here's the cement," she said as she put the sacks in Muck's front scoop.

"Thanks, Wendy!" he called.

Pilchard licked her lips and moved closer to the bucket. Wendy loosened what was left of the wooden support and tied some rope tightly around it.

"Right, now, Lofty. It's your turn! Can you help me pull the broken stump out of the ground?" asked Wendy.

"Oh, er... yes... I think so," muttered Lofty as he swung his hook into place.

"OK, pull!" called Wendy. And Lofty began to heave. While Wendy was busy, Pilchard placed her front paws on the bucket and watched Finn. She was just about to dip a paw into the water when the stump came free.

"Well done, Lofty!" cried Wendy.

But Lofty had trouble controlling his arm and the stump flew towards Pilchard.

"**Yeeoow!**" yelped Pilchard as she ran away.

Wendy found Bob's drill and climbed the ladder to fasten the new wooden post to the roof.

Pilchard saw that Wendy was busy, and crept up to the bucket again. She put her paws on the edge and peered down at Finn.

When Bob arrived back at the yard Wendy was still up the ladder. Pilchard ran and hid behind Scoop.

"There, all done!" Wendy said, climbing down.
"Hello, Wendy," called Bob. "What are
you up to?"
"Ummm," she said.
"Err... I had a little accident, Bob,"
said Muck, owning up.
"It wasn't his fault," added Scoop.
"I skidded to miss Bird and I bashed right
into the lean-to," explained Muck.

"Sorry, Bob," said Muck.
"There's no need to be sorry. You didn't do it on purpose and Bird's fine," said Bob.
"It's as good as new!" said Bob as he and Muck inspected the lean-to. "Wendy, our brilliant builder, has fixed it!"
"I couldn't have done it without Lofty's help!" Wendy said.

While everyone was looking at Muck and the mended
lean-to, Pilchard crept back to the bucket.
This time she was determined to catch Finn. She
dipped her paw into the water... but
Bird was on top of the lean-to and
spotted Pilchard. He gave a loud,
"Toot, toot!" to catch
everyone's attention.
"Weeeeooow!" yelped
Pilchard as she jumped back and
ran away.

Wendy heard the commotion and rushed over.

"Oh, Pilchard! Bird! I'd completely forgotten about poor Finn!" said Wendy as she reached down to stroke Pilchard. "What a clever cat and what a clever bird!"

"There's been so much excitement with the lean-to, I'd forgotten I was cleaning out the fish tank. But Pilchard and Bird just reminded me," said Wendy.

"Miaow!" said Pilchard, crossly.

"There you go, Finn. All nice and clean again," said Bob, as he scooped up Finn from the bucket and dropped him into the tank. Pilchard prowled around the sitting room.

"Pilchard!" called Wendy. "I've got a little reward for you, for being such a clever cat. Look, a lovely fish for your tea!"

Pilchard had had quite enough of fish for one day and sunk to the floor.

"**Miaow, wowww, wiaoww!**" she moaned.

"I wonder what's up with Pilchard," puzzled Bob.

"At least Finn's pleased," said Wendy, as Finn did a perfect backflip in his lovely clean tank.

THE END!

Lofty to the Rescue

Bob and the team were mending the holes in a country road, but they had to stop when they came to a bridge that was blocked with logs and bricks.
"Oh dear! We'll have to clear this before we can get to work on the road," said Bob.
"**Can we clear it?**" asked Scoop.
"**Yes, we can!**" cried Bob, Dizzy and Lofty.

Everyone got straight to work clearing the bridge, except for Lofty.

"Errrr," I'm scared of heights he said, looking at the bridge nervously.

"I think I'll find another way round," he said as he started to back away.

Spud jumped out from behind a bush, "Hee, hee! Lofty's scared of heights!" he teased.

"Hey, Spud," called Scoop. "Stop it! Leave him alone."

But Spud ignored him, and started to make mud pies to throw at Lofty.

"Neh, neh, neh! Lofty's a scaredy-crane!" he called as Lofty set off.

Spud jumped up and down calling after Lofty, but then he slipped... wobbled... and fell, right out over the side of the bridge.

"**Woooaaaaahhhhhhh!**" he shouted.

Luckily, Spud didn't fall too far. His trousers caught on a branch that was sticking out. The machines gathered around him.

"Help!" he screamed.

"How are we going to rescue him?" asked Muck.

"The only one who can reach that far is Lofty," said Scoop.

"Hang in there, Spud. I'll try and catch up with Lofty," shouted Muck as he set off as fast as he could.

Muck managed to find Lofty.
  "Please come and help,"
begged Muck.
  "Spud was very unkind. But if he's
in trouble, I suppose I'd better," said
Lofty, looking very worried. They went
back to the bridge and the other machines
watched nervously.
  Suddenly the branch made a loud, **Crack!**
  "You'll have to be quick, Lofty," said Bob. "Lower your
jib. Gently does it!"
  "Ohhh, I can't look," whimpered Lofty. "Bob, you'll
have to tell me what to do."

"**Oh, ohhhh!**" wailed Spud as the branch began to give way under his weight.

"Forward a bit, Lofty," Bob called. "Now lower your hook."

Lofty edged his hook closer to Spud, and slipped it through his belt.

Then, very carefully, Lofty wound up his line and placed Spud safely back on the ground.

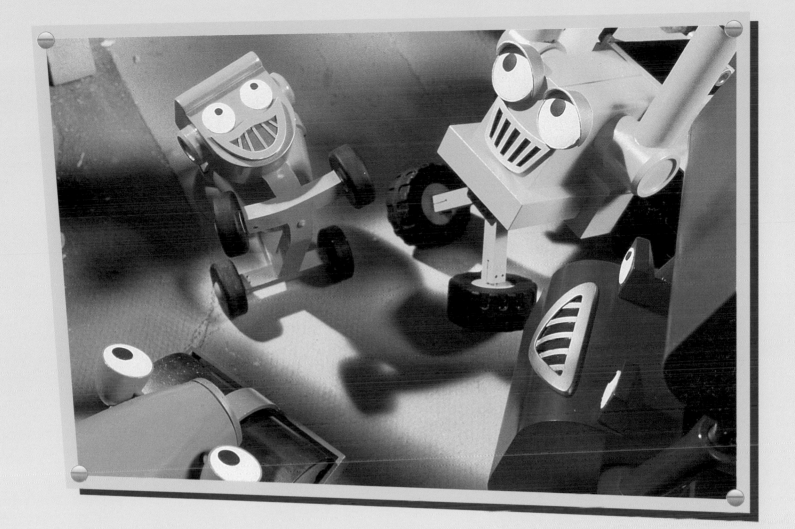

The rest of the team watched from below the bridge until Spud was lifted safely back onto the bridge.

"**Hooray!**" they all cheered when the rescue was over.

"Nice one, Lofty," said Scoop.

"Oh? Did I do it?" asked Lofty.

"Of course you did, Lofty. You can open your eyes now," said Bob. "I think Spud has something to say to you, don't you Spud?"

"Er, yeah. Thanks, Lofty, and sorry about teasing you," said Spud.

Lofty opened his eyes to find everyone grinning at him. "You've saved the day, Lofty!" said Bob. Lofty smiled. He wasn't such a scaredy-crane after all!

THE END!

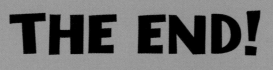

Bob's Bugle

Bob the Builder was busy mending a broken central heating system. Muck was helping him.

"I've finished the boiler," said Bob coming downstairs. "Now for the new hot water tank."

Muck helped Bob get the tank out of his back tipper and the pipes from his front scoop. Bob quickly fixed them to the boiler.

"Now it's time to check the pipes," he said.

One of the pipes was blocked by a little bit of dirt.
Bob blew down the pipe and the dirt popped out.
Bleurgh-boo-boo-blooooh! whistled the pipe,
as Bob blew through it.

"I like that," laughed Bob.

"Bob? Are you all right in there?" called
Muck, anxiously.

"Yes, I'm fine," Bob replied. "Listen to
this, Muck."

T-o-o-o-o-t-tee-toooot-tooot!

"What is it... a frog with a sore throat?" Muck asked.

"No!" said Bob, excitedly. "It's my bugle! Or it will be, when I've finished making it."

"What's a bugle?" Muck asked on the way back to the yard.

"It's a musical instrument," Bob explained. "You blow in one end and a loud noise comes out of the other. Listen!" and he gave another blast down the pipe.

Parrrrrp-tee-ti-tee toooot-tooooot!

Back at the yard, Wendy was looking
very thoughtful.

"Some friends of mine have just moved
into a new house and I'd really like to
give them something special. But I can't
think of anything!" Wendy told Lofty.
Pilchard pushed her clockwork mouse
towards Wendy.

"That's very kind," Wendy said. "But I don't
think my friends really need a clockwork mouse."
Then Muck and Bob roared into the yard.

"Guess what?" Muck yelled. "Bob's going to make
a bugle!"

Bob hurried into his workshop and shut the door. The machines clustered around outside. They could hear interesting bangs and clanks. Then suddenly a loud **parp!** made them all jump.

"How about this, then?" Bob said, as he came out waving his new bugle. He put it to his mouth and blew.

Bloohoooowoopaarp!

"What's that awful noise?" cried Wendy, rushing out of her office with her hands clamped over her ears.

"Shhh, Wendy," whispered Scoop. "It's Bob's new bugle and he thinks it's brilliant."

"It's terrible!" cried Wendy.

"It's great!" rumbled Roley.

"Really?" chuckled Bob. "Perhaps I could join a band!"

"You'll have to practise hard," said Roley.

"You're right," agreed Bob. **"Can I practise? Yes, I can!"** he shouted.

Bob practised his bugle all night long.
Blooo-hooo-dooo-diddley-diddley-dooo!
"I want to go to sleep!" wailed Muck.
"Perhaps we should say something to Bob?"
Lofty mumbled.
"Bob's just having fun!" rumbled Roley.
The tired machines listened as the
loud bugle blasts slowly turned to
weak **toot-toots**, then one last
paaaarp.
"He's stopped!" gasped Dizzy.
"Thank goodness for that,"
yawned Muck.

"I hardly slept last night, worrying about what present to get my friends," Wendy said looking at the list that she'd written.

"We hardly slept last night because of Bob playing his bugle!" grumbled Muck.

"He'll be tired this morning," said Wendy.

But Bob wasn't the slightest bit tired. He strolled across the yard, playing his bugle. The terrible noise sounded like an elephant blowing its nose.

"Come on, Muck! We've got work to do," Bob said as he put his bugle by the door of the workshop.

"Now's our chance, Lofty!" said Scoop. "Grab the bugle!"

"Woaahh," Lofty gulped as he extended his jib and hooked the bugle onto the end.

"Bob will never find it on the roof," Dizzy said.

Carefully, Lofty put it on the roof. But then Bird hopped over to the bugle and started to peck at it. The bugle rolled forwards.

"Look out!" cried Muck. The bugle rolled off the roof and landed in his scoop.

"What was that?" called Bob, coming out of the workshop.

"Nothing!" said Muck.

"Come on, Muck," said Bob. "We've got to finish that central heating job."

While Bob packed the last of his tools, Muck hunted around for somewhere to hide the bugle. Dizzy ran up to him and tipped her mixer forwards.

"Stick it in here," she whispered.

"Phew… what a relief," sighed Muck. But then disaster struck!

"Dizzy," called Bob. "I'll need you, too!"

Dizzy's face dropped, "Me!" she exclaimed. "Oh no!"

At the house, Bob went inside to fix the radiators, singing as he worked.

Outside, Dizzy and Muck wondered what to do.

"Can't you just leave the bugle somewhere?" asked Muck.

"I can't do that!" protested Dizzy.

Suddenly, Bob appeared at the door with a bucket.

"Cement please, Dizzy," he said.

"Are you sure?" gulped Dizzy.

"Of course I'm sure!" laughed Bob.

"Here goes…" sighed Dizzy. She poured a load of cement into Bob's bucket. **Glug-glug-CLANG!**

Bob couldn't believe his eyes when he saw his bugle covered in cement.

"How did that get in there?" he cried.

Muck and Dizzy pretended to be surprised.

"I've no idea!" squeaked Dizzy.

"Me, neither," said Muck, firmly.

"Oh, well," said Bob. "No harm done. I'll soon have it cleaned up."

Back at the yard Bob wiped the sticky concrete off his bugle. Then he put it on the ground in front of the workshop while he called Roley.

"Can you come over here, Roley?" he said.

"OK, Bob," rumbled Roley, as he moved forwards.

But he didn't look where he was going.

There was a terrible **crunch!** Roley had rolled right over Bob's bugle.

41

"What was that noise?" asked Bob.

Roley stared down at the flattened bugle.

"It's your bugle, Bob," he groaned. "I'm so sorry... I've flattened it!"

Although Bob felt sad, he could see that Roley was really very upset.

"Don't worry, Roley," he said. "I shouldn't have left it lying around like that."

He bent down to pick up the flattened bugle.

Tinkle... tinkle... tinkle... went the broken pieces.

"That's a lovely set of wind chimes," said Wendy, coming out of her office. "Just the sort of house-warming present I have been looking for."

Bob smiled at the wind chimes dangling in his hand.

"You know, there I was, thinking I'd made a bugle, when it was really a set of wind chimes! Here you are, Wendy, you can have these for your friends."

"Thank you, Bob," cried Wendy. She gently shook the chimes. **Tinkle... tinkle... tinkle...**

"Ah..." sighed Muck, "nice, quiet wind chimes."

"I quite liked the bugle myself!" rumbled Roley.

THE END!

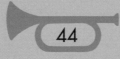

Wallpaper Wendy

We're off to re-lay the road in front of the town hall. Is everyone ready?" asked Bob.

"**Can I roll it?**" asked Roley.

"**Yes, you can!**" shouted Muck. Dizzy didn't hear because she was listening to music on her headphones.

"Come on, Dizzy," said Wendy. "Bob will need your help, too!"

When they got to the town hall, Bob and Muck shovelled the gravel into place.

"OK, Roley," said Muck. "We're ready for you to do your bit."

"Rock and roooll!" shouted Roley as he moved forward and crunched the gravel flat.

Mrs Broadbent stood watching the team working. When they stopped for a break, she rushed over to speak to Bob.

"Bob, can you help?" she asked. "My mother is arriving tomorrow and the flat isn't ready. My decorators have let me down."

"Bob, you're a builder, not a decorator," warned Muck.

"Decorating's easy!" said Bob, **"Can we fix it?"**

"Err...Yes, we can!" all the machines answered. But they weren't sure!

Bob and Dizzy went over to Mrs Broadbent's flat straightaway. They didn't have much time, so they got to work as quickly as they could.

Bob tried to put paste on the wallpaper but it wouldn't lie flat! It stuck to his hands and to the ladder but not to the wall.

Then, as Bob climbed down the ladder, he put his foot straight into the bucket of paste!

Dizzy tried to get Bob's foot out of the bucket, but she couldn't stop herself laughing. She slipped on some paste and the bucket flew up in the air and landed on Bob's head!

"This isn't as easy as I thought it would be," complained Bob.

Wendy arrived just in time.

"Bob! Dizzy! What are you doing?" exclaimed Wendy. "Look at all this mess!"

"You'd better go and get some lunch and I'll see what I can do here," said Wendy.

She cleaned and washed. Then she pasted and papered. Soon the room looked lovely. Just as she finished painting the radiator, she heard a noise at the front door.

It was Mrs Broadbent coming to see how the team were getting on. Bob arrived back from lunch at the same time.

"Hello, Mrs Broadbent. I was just telling the machines how well it was all going," said Bob, guiltily. "But you can't go in. It's not... er... quite ready yet," he mumbled, remembering the mess.

But Mrs Broadbent went in anyway...

Bob was surprised to see the wallpaper
up and the room neat and tidy!
"Wow!" he said.
Mrs Broadbent was thrilled!
"You've done a fabulous job, Bob.
You're so clever!" she said.
"Oh, don't thank me," said Bob.
"Wendy did it all. She's brilliant!"

THE END!

Roley's Tortoise

The team were working on a lay-by for a new bus stop in the country.

"Right, Muck! We're ready for the hardcore," said Wendy.

"OK! Where do you want it?" said Muck, eagerly, as he rolled forward.

"Over here, please," she replied, pointing at a spot just in front of Roley.

Muck lowered his scoop and dumped
the hardcore. Wendy waved Roley
forward to flatten it.
"Come on, Bird! Let's rock
and roll!" rumbled Roley.
"**Toot!**" cheeped Bird, happily.

Dizzy was practising her aerobics routine, "...to the left... two, three, four and **stre-e-etch**," she chanted. As she reached up she noticed something moving just in front of Roley.

"Stop, Roley! Stop!" Dizzy shouted. Roley concentrated really hard and screeched to a halt.

"What is it, Dizzy?" asked Bob.

"Look!" said Dizzy. "There's a stone with a head and it's moving!"

"Wow! It's a tortoise," Wendy said. "How on earth did it get here?"

"It's a good job you spotted him, Dizzy. We could have had a very nasty accident," said Wendy.

"Yeah," said Dizzy, smiling proudly.

The tortoise started to climb the pile of hardcore very slowly. Bird jumped down.

Roley peered down at the tortoise.

"You're like me, aren't you?" he said.

"Slow, but you get there in the end. What are we going to do with him, Wendy?"

"I don't know, Roley, but he can't stay here while we're working, he might get hurt," Wendy replied.

"Can I take Timmy back to the yard, please?" Roley begged.

"Who's Timmy?" asked Bob.

"Timmy the tortoise… that's his name!" said Roley.

"Ha, ha!" laughed Bob. "Yes, we'll keep him until we find his owner," said Bob. He picked up Timmy to keep him safe, while Roley finished the job. When the lay-by was nice and flat, Bob, Roley and Dizzy took Timmy back to the yard.

Muck went on ahead to collect the material for the bus stop with Lofty.

"I've got the shelter, so can you carry the bus stop sign?" Muck called over to Lofty.

"Oh… er… yeah, I think so…" said Lofty and he followed Muck back to the lay-by.

At the yard, Bob, Dizzy, Scoop, Bird and Roley gathered around Timmy's box.

"Awww! Can we keep him, Bob?" asked Dizzy.

"Tortoises are an endangered species. Timmy must be very precious to someone. We'll have to find his owner," said Bob.

"Timmy's owner will be looking everywhere for him," said Scoop.

"You're right, Scoop," said Bob. "I want you and Dizzy to go and find out if any of the neighbours have lost a tortoise."

"**Can we find them?**" shouted Bob.

"**Yes, we can!**" Scoop and Dizzy replied, as they rushed out of the yard and began knocking on all the doors in the street.

Meanwhile Roley watched over Timmy as he nibbled on a lettuce leaf.

Dizzy trundled off to Mrs Potts's house. When she arrived
Mrs Potts was in her garden searching under the bushes.

"Tommy, Tommy!" she called.

"Have you lost something?" asked Dizzy.

"Yes, my tortoise," she replied.

"Oh, we've found him!" cried Dizzy.

"Thank goodness. Is he all right?"
Mrs Potts asked.

"Yes! Come to the yard and see,"
said Dizzy jumping up and down.

At the bus stop, Wendy was digging a hole for the signpost when Lofty and Muck arrived with the rest of the bits for the bus shelter.

"Well done! Now, gently does it, Lofty," she instructed, as he lifted a piece of the shelter from Muck's back dumper and placed it by the signpost.

"Now for the roof," said Wendy. Lofty lifted the roof panel very slowly.

"Forward a bit," Wendy called to Lofty.

"Careful!" shouted Muck as Lofty swung the panel over his head.

"**Can we build it?**" asked Wendy.

"**Yes, we can!**" Lofty and Muck shouted back.

"Good work, team," said Wendy when Lofty had put the final piece in place.

Back at the yard, Roley was guarding Timmy's box. But soon he began to get tired...

"Arrrghh!" he yawned as he fell asleep. Bird and Pilchard snuck up to Timmy's box. Pilchard tipped the box over to get a closer look. Timmy poked his head and legs out of his shell. Pilchard got such a fright she ran to the other side of the yard.

Bird watched the tortoise start to move away, slowly.

"Toot, toot," he said as he jumped up onto Timmy's shell, trying to stop him from escaping, but Timmy carried on out of the yard! Roley was still fast asleep.

Bob met Farmer Pickles and Travis outside the yard.

"Hello, Farmer Pickles. That's a lovely load of lettuces you've got there," he said.

"We're on our way to sell them at the market," said Farmer Pickles.

Bird jumped on top of the trailer of lettuces. Some of them wobbled and fell onto the pavement.

"Whoops! Be careful, Bird!" said Bob.

"Don't worry, Travis, I'll pick them up for you," Bob said as he scooped up the lettuces.

He didn't realise that he'd picked up Timmy as well! When Bob put them on Travis's trailer, he put Timmy on the pile too.

"Do you think I could keep a lettuce for the tortoise we've found?" Bob asked.

"Yes, of course," said Farmer Pickles as he climbed up onto Travis.

Roley was looking at Timmy's empty box when Dizzy and Mrs Potts arrived at the yard.

"Where's my tortoise?" Mrs Potts asked.

"I don't know. I think Timmy's lost!" said Roley sadly. "I fell asleep and when I woke up, he was gone."

"He's called Tommy, Roley," Mrs Potts corrected.

Everyone searched all over the yard. Apart from Roley who kept very still just in case he rolled over the tortoise.

"**Tooooommyyy!**" called Dizzy.

Wendy, Muck and Lofty arrived back at the yard and joined in the search. Farmer Pickles followed them in.

"I might have found just what you're looking for," he said. "He was fast asleep at the bottom of the trailer."

"Oh, thank you, Farmer Pickles," said Mrs Potts.

Bob and Roley helped take the tortoise back to Mrs Potts's house.

"This new run should keep Timmy... err, Tommy, safely off the roads," said Bob.

"I thought he looked like a Timmy, but now I think he's more of a Tommy!" laughed Roley.

"I'm just glad to have him back," said Mrs Potts.

67

"It's been a busy day," said Scoop.

"Yeah, we built a great bus stop, didn't we, Lofty?" said Muck.

"Er, yeah… I think so," Lofty replied.

"I found a tortoise," added Roley.

"And I found it's owner," chirped Dizzy.

"Aww, I'm going to miss that little fella," said Roley. "But I'm glad he's back with Mrs Potts where he belongs."

THE END!

Naughty Spud

Spud was gazing up at an apple tree. The apples looked juicy and ready to eat. But he couldn't quite reach them! He jumped as high as he could, but it wasn't high enough.

"Hmm…" he muttered as he tried to work out a way of getting the apples off the tree.

Just then, Travis trundled past.

"Guess what?" he said excitedly. "Bob is going to finish building my shed today. I can't wait. It'll be so cosy."

Bob was at Farmer Pickles's farm, nailing the roof of Travis's shed in place.

"Nearly done," Bob called down to Dizzy. "We can go home soon."

But Dizzy didn't hear. She was busy listening to the music on her headphones!

Spud walked by and spotted Bob's ladder.

"Perfect!" he whispered to himself. No one was watching, so he decided to borrow it.

Bob had nearly finished the roof when Muck turned up.
Dizzy was still singing to herself and didn't notice
Muck arrive.

"Muck, where's the ladder?" called Bob.

"I can't see it anywhere," Muck replied.

"Oh, no! I'm stuck up here! How am
I going to get down?" moaned Bob.

Spud propped the ladder against the trunk
of the tree and climbed up. Soon he had
picked every single apple on the
tree! He got to work eating
the huge pile of fruit.
"Hmm, delicious!" he mumbled
through a mouthful of apple.

Bob used his mobile to ring Wendy, and she and Scoop
set off to Farmer Pickles's farm straightaway.
"Can we rescue him?" asked Wendy.
"Yes, we can!" shouted Scoop.
Bob was really relieved to see
Wendy and Scoop.

"Thank goodness you're
here," he sighed. "I was
beginning to think I
would have to sleep
up here tonight!"

Scoop raised his front scoop up towards Bob.
  "Don't worry, Bob," said Wendy. "We'll soon have
you down."
  "Jump in my front scoop," cried Scoop.
  Bob climbed in carefully and Scoop
lowered him to the ground very gently.
  "Thank you," Bob beamed.
"I wonder who took my ladder?"

Just then, Spud appeared, clutching his
stomach. He'd eaten far too many apples!
   "Spud, have you seen my ladder?"
asked Bob.
   "Well, I... er, needed a ladder to
reach some apples," mumbled Spud.
   "Oh, Spud! Bob's been stuck on
that roof all afternoon," said Wendy.
   "Ohhh! Now I've got a horrible
stomachache," moaned Spud.
   "Well it serves you right for being
so greedy," Wendy told him. "Go and
get that ladder now, before you get into any
more mischief!"

That night Spud had a very sore tummy. He went to see Travis.

Travis was so happy and warm in his new shed, that he felt a bit sorry for Spud.

"Travis, if I bring you the rest of the apples, can I stay in your shed tonight?" begged Spud.

"I suppose so," Travis laughed. "But I hope you've learned your lesson!"

THE END!

Travis Paints the Town

Wendy was busy giving out the jobs for the day. "Bob," she called. "You, Muck and Roley are off to finish the new section of road. Travis can follow you with the road-marking machine in his trailer."

"What's a road-marking machine?" asked Muck.

"It's a machine that paints lines down the middle of a new road," Bob explained.

"It's important to keep the line straight, so that cars can travel either side of it and don't bump into each other," added Wendy.

The team set off for the new section of road. When they got there, Roley thundered up and down, flattening every bump in sight.

"When you've finished, we can start painting the road," said Bob.

The busy machines didn't notice that Spud was peeping at them from behind a bush in a nearby field.

"This looks like a lot of fun!" he chuckled.

Bob pushed the road-marking machine into the middle of the road and loaded it with thick white paint. Just as he was about to start painting lines, his mobile phone rang.

"Hello, Mrs Potts!" he said. "Really? No, don't worry, I'll pop over right away!"

"What's up, Bob?" rumbled Roley.

"Mrs Potts's fence is broken and she doesn't want her dog to get out," Bob replied. "I'd better go over there. It won't take me long to fix it."

"OK, we'll wait here," said Roley.

Bob jumped onto Muck and roared off down the road.

Travis, Roley and Bird stood in the sunshine waiting for Bob. They didn't see Spud pop up from behind a bush and creep towards the road-marking machine. Very quietly, he dragged the machine behind Travis. He unhooked the empty trailer and attached the road-marking machine in its place! Then he slipped back to the bushes.
"Tee-hee!" he giggled. "Now, for some fun!"

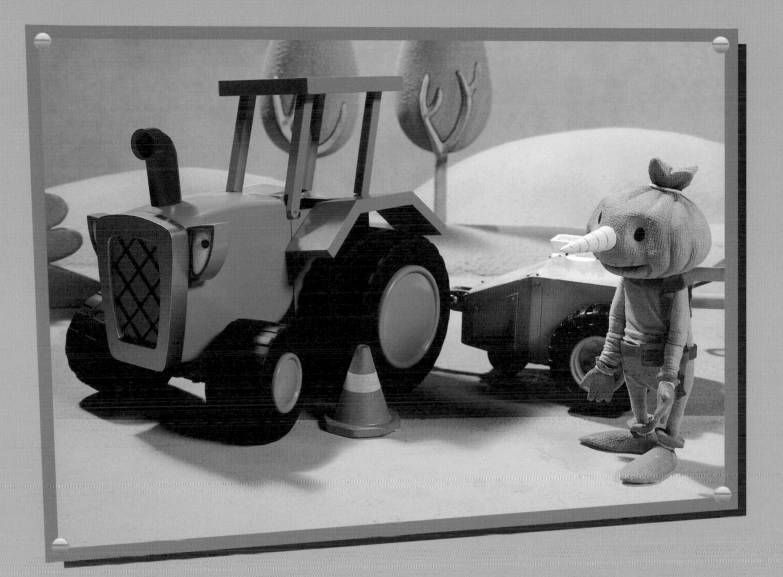

Spud walked out, whistling loudly, as if he had just arrived.

"Hi, Travis!" he called. "I've got a message for you! Farmer Pickles wants you down at the pond. It's really important."

"I'd better get going," said Travis as he roared off, pulling the road-marking machine behind him!

As Travis hurried on his way, the road-marking machine bounced along after him, painting wiggly lines all over the new road.

"Stop, Travis! Come back!" Roley bellowed when he saw what was happening. "Come on, Bird! We've got to stop him!"

From behind the bush, naughty Spud rocked with laughter as Roley lumbered off after Travis.

"This is the best fun ever!" Spud laughed.

Travis rushed to the duck pond as fast as his wheels could turn. He was so determined to get there as quickly as possible, that he didn't spot Farmer Pickles working in a field next to the country lane. He whizzed straight past him.

"Oh, dear!" gasped Farmer Pickles when he saw the wiggly white lines trailing behind Travis.

When Roley and Bird came along, Farmer Pickles called to them, "Follow that tractor!"

Wendy was in the office when Farmer Pickles phoned.

"Dear me, white paint everywhere!" she cried. "Don't worry, I'll tell Bob right away!"

Bob was busy hammering the last nail into Mrs Potts's fence.

"There you go," he said. "That should keep your dog nice and safe!"

"Thank you," said Mrs Potts, smiling with relief.

"No problem," said Bob, as his mobile phone rang. "Hi, Wendy. What? Travis? Paint everywhere? I'm on my way!" he said.

Travis was a lot lighter than Roley and a lot faster, too!
The poor steamroller panted and spluttered as he
trundled along after Travis with Farmer Pickles and
Bird on board.

"**Travis!**" yelled Farmer Pickles, at the
top of his voice. But Travis still couldn't
hear them over the roar of his engine.

He raced along the road. As he went
faster and faster, the white lines he
painted got wigglier and wigglier!

While Roley and Farmer Pickles struggled to catch up with Travis, Bob and Muck were chasing after him, too.

"Quick as you can," urged Bob. "We've got to stop him before he paints the whole town white!"

"I don't think I can go any faster!" spluttered Muck as he revved up his engine.

"Please try, Muck," cried Bob. "Please try!"

Travis zoomed along the road and started to head across a field towards the duck pond.

Spud peeped out from behind a bush to admire the mess.

"Hee, hee, hee!" he chuckled. "Now Travis is painting the grass white, too!"

Then poor, tired Roley wheezed past him. His heavy machinery clattered and rattled as he trundled after Travis.

Spud chased after them all, laughing all the way.

Bob and Muck raced down the hill, towards the
duck pond at the bottom.

"Watch out, Muck!" Bob yelled as he saw Travis
heading straight for them. Muck tried to avoid the
tractor. He slammed on his brakes and screeched to
a stop to try to miss Travis.

"**Help!**" roared Travis, swerving sideways. The
road-marking machine zig-zagged behind him,
then came unhooked. It rolled down the road, skidded
sideways and turned over…

Farmer Pickles and Roley were next to arrive. There was thick white paint spilled everywhere!

Everyone stared at the puddle of wet paint.

"Just look at this mess," Bob groaned.

Poor Travis was very upset.

"I didn't know the road-marking machine was hooked onto me. I don't even know how it got there!" he said.

"I tried my best to stop him, Bob," panted Roley. "But I couldn't catch him."

"Spud told me you needed me right away," Travis explained to Farmer Pickles.

"I didn't say that!" said Farmer Pickles.

Behind them, a bush started to shake with laughter.

"Spud!" yelled Farmer Pickles.

Spud peeped nervously over the bush.

"What have you been up to?" Farmer Pickles asked.

"Me? Nothing!" Spud replied, trying to look innocent.

"So who hooked the road-marker onto Travis?" Bob demanded.

"Um… it was me," Spud confessed, hanging his head.

"You've got some cleaning up to do," Farmer Pickles said to the naughty scarecrow. He got a big bucket, filled it with soapy water and gave Spud a big scrubbing brush.
"Off you go," he said. "And keep scrubbing until it's all cleaned up."

Spud scrubbed and... scrubbed... and scrubbed. On his aching knees, he followed the wiggly lines all along the country lanes.
He cleaned up every spot of white paint.
By the time Spud had finished it was really late and it was getting dark.

"**Can Spud scrub it?**"
"**Yes, he can!**" Spud said to himself as he set off for home.

THE END!

Dizzy's Birdwatch

"Hey, everyone!" Bob called one morning. "Come and have a look at this! It's a bird's nest! And there's an egg!"

"And here comes the mother," said Wendy.

"We'll have to make sure that no one disturbs the nest, so that the egg can hatch into a baby bird," said Bob.

"Dizzy, I won't be needing any cement today, so why don't you stay here and birdwatch?" said Bob.

"**Yesss!**" cried Dizzy.

"Can we birdwatch, too?" pleaded Muck and Lofty.

"I'm sorry, but we've got a big roofing job today. Lofty, I'll need you to carry the tiles," said Bob.

"**Can we fix it?**" asked Bob.

"**Yes, we can!**" Muck, Scoop and Lofty shouted.

Dizzy watched the egg very carefully.

"Don't worry, Mummy Bird. I'm going to look after you and your egg, because I'm your egg's auntie!" she told the bird.

Wendy came out of her office to see how Dizzy was getting on.

"Oh, Dizzy, you're a great birdwatcher!" she said.

Pilchard came over to join Dizzy. They sat very quietly and watched the bird. Nothing seemed to be happening so they decided to have a game of football.

"Dizzy beats the defender," shouted Dizzy. "It's a goal!" she cried as she pushed the ball into the corner. Wendy rushed over and just managed to stop the ball knocking over the nest.

"Phew! That was close! You nearly disturbed the egg," she warned.

Dizzy and Pilchard left the football and went back to watch the egg.

"Look! The baby bird is hatching," cried Dizzy.

"Squawk," croaked the mummy bird, proudly.

"Ohhh, he's so sweet," whispered Dizzy.

"Wendy, Wendy! Come quickly!" shouted Dizzy. "The egg has hatched. And look, the baby bird is so small!"

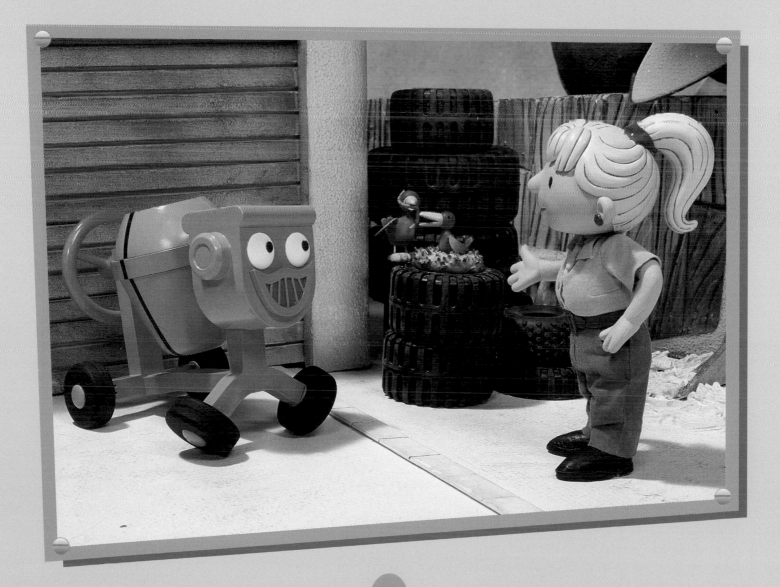

The mummy bird fed the baby bird juicy worms every day, and every day the baby bird grew bigger and stronger.

"Ahhh, isn't he growing fast?" said Dizzy.

"Yes," said Wendy. "I don't think it will be long before he leaves the nest."

Dizzy was sad. She didn't want the baby bird to leave.

"You're just in time to see something really special,"
Wendy said to Scoop and Dizzy, one day. "I think the baby
bird is going to fly!"

The baby bird tottered on the edge of the pile of tyres,
then jumped off... but he fell
to the ground! Scoop
picked him up and put him
back in the nest. The baby
bird tried again. He
flapped his wings and
this time, he glided up
into the sky!

"**Wow!**" cried Scoop
and Dizzy together.

When Bob and the other machines came back, they were just in time to see the baby bird practising.

Suddenly, the baby bird swooped onto Dizzy's head and chirped loudly.

"I think he's saying thank you and goodbye," said Wendy.

"That's OK! It was fun birdsitting you," laughed Dizzy.

"Bye!" shouted the team, as the baby bird followed its mummy. They flew out of the yard and off into the countryside.

THE END!

Wendy's Busy Day

One cold Monday morning, Wendy found
Bob wrapped in a blanket by the fire.
"**A-a-a-a-a-choo!**" he sneezed.
"Goodness, you look ill!" cried Wendy.
"I've dot a really bad dold!" sniffed Bob.
"You'd better stay at home," said Wendy.
"I can't do that!" spluttered Bob. "We've dot
a big road resurfacing job to do and it's dot
to be finished by five o'clock tonight."

"Why don't I do it?" said Wendy. "Otherwise it won't get done at all."

"Thank you… **A-a-a-choo!**" sneezed Bob.

"I'll tell the machines," said Wendy as she headed out of the door.

Pilchard pushed her food dish forwards.

"Miaow!" she mewed.

"I dow you want your breakfast," Bob told her, "but I…" Bob stopped as another huge sneeze tickled his nose.

"Miaow!" yowled Pilchard, hungrily.

"Bob's got a very bad cold," Wendy told the machines. "So, he's going to stay indoors until he gets better."

"How will we do the resurfacing without Bob?" fretted Lofty.

"You've got me!" smiled Wendy.

"Hurray!" cheered the machines.

"Right, I'll stay behind to look after Bob," said Scoop.

"Me, too," said Lofty, shyly.

Wendy hopped up onto Muck's step.

"**Can we fix it?**" she called.

"**Yes, we can!**" yelled the team.

Wendy gulped with surprise when she saw the big potholes in the road.

"Oh, dear, it's very bumpy," she said.

Roley chuckled. "Hey, Wendy, flattening bumps is my job!" he said.

"OK!" smiled Wendy. "Let's do it!"

Back at home, Bob sat sneezing. "Are you feeling better?" called Scoop, from outside the window. "I feel dewwible!" wheezed Bob.

On the town road, Dizzy mixed concrete to fill in the potholes.

Then Muck roared up.

"Here it comes," he yelled, as he lifted his dumper to tip out the sticky road surface.

"I'm right behind you!" rumbled Roley, as he moved in to flatten it out.

S-Q-U-E-L-C-H!

Wendy beamed and clapped.
"That looks perfect!" she cried.

As Dizzy moved over to give Roley more room, she spotted an old football lying by the side of the road.

"Oooh! Look what I've found!" she squeaked, excitedly. "...and Dizzy's got the ball," she cried, as she chased after it. "She's racing down the wing. Is she going to score?"

"No! Stop!" yelled Wendy, as Dizzy headed for the sticky, wet road surface. Dizzy didn't hear.

"She's scored!" shouted Dizzy as she landed **splat** in the sticky stuff.

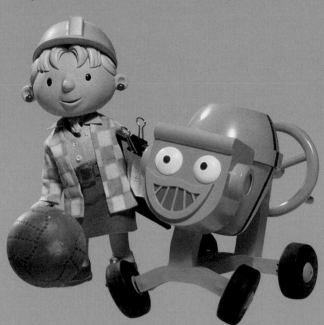

"Awww!" wailed Dizzy, as she watched her wheels slowly sinking. "I'm stuck!"

"Don't worry!" gasped Wendy. "We'll get you out!"

"How? If we go in there we'll get stuck as well," rumbled Roley.

"You can't just leave me here to set like a rock!" shrieked Dizzy.

"Oh, dear," said Wendy. "Let's think about this carefully."

"We can't go **in**," she reasoned. "But Dizzy has to be pulled **out**..."

"I've got an idea!" roared Muck. "Let's get Lofty. He'll pull Dizzy out in a flash!"

"We've got to be quick though," added Muck as he whizzed back to the yard with Wendy.

"Lofty! Scoop!" Muck yelled as he screeched to a halt.

"You two are back early," said Lofty, in surprise.

"Lofty! We need your help!" cried Wendy.

"Dizzy's stuck in some sticky stuff and we need you to pull her out!" chugged Muck.

"Err... OK. Lofty to the rescue!" called Lofty.
As the machines revved out of the yard, Bob woke up.
"Scoop!" Bob called. "What was all that noise? And where's Lofty gone?"
Scoop wriggled uncomfortably.
"Oh, er... he went to see how the others are getting on," he replied.
"Oh, dear," Bob sighed. "I hope everything is going smoothly."

Things weren't going at all smoothly at the new road. Lofty lowered his big metal hook towards Dizzy's handle. "Get a grip, Dizzy!" he clanked. "Got it!" squeaked Dizzy. **"Pull!"** As Lofty pulled Dizzy up, he lost his grip and Dizzy crashed to the ground. "Try again!" yelled Dizzy, crossly. Wendy, Roley and Muck held their breath as they watched Lofty strain and heave.

Slowly, Lofty hauled Dizzy free of the concrete.

"Yes!" squealed Dizzy, as he gently lowered her
down onto the ground.

"Hooray for Lofty!" cheered Wendy.

"Thank you," giggled Dizzy in relief.

Wendy looked at her watch, "Oh,
goodness. We've only got half
an hour left to finish the road! We'll
have to work really hard."

The machines worked as quickly as
they could.

With Wendy supervising, Muck tipped the last load
of road surface onto the road for Roley to flatten.
DONG! DONG! DONG! DONG! DONG!
"Five o'clock!" yelled Wendy. "Time to open the road!"
Quickly, Lofty cleared away the safety barriers. Everyone
gathered around the tape blocking off the road.
"I pronounce this road open!" said Wendy in a loud
voice. And she snipped through the tape with a pair
of scissors.
"**Hooray!**" cheered the tired machines.

The first vehicle to use the resurfaced road was Travis,
with Spud perched on the side.

"We've just mended the road!" squeaked
Dizzy, excitedly.

Spud inspected the road.

"You've missed a bit," he said.

"Where?" asked Dizzy.

"It looks perfect to me," said
Wendy, anxiously.

"Only teasing," laughed Spud.
"It looks perfect to me, too! Hah,
hah, hah!"

Back at the yard, Bob hurried out to meet everybody.

"We did it, Bob!" called Wendy.

"Wad a deam!" croaked Bob. "Dank you all so much."

"Um… it's cold out here," fretted Lofty. "Shouldn't you get back indoors, Bob?"

"Better do as you're told," teased Wendy.

"OK," laughed Bob. "I'll have an early night."

Wendy yawned an enormous yawn.

"We'll **all** need an early night," she said.

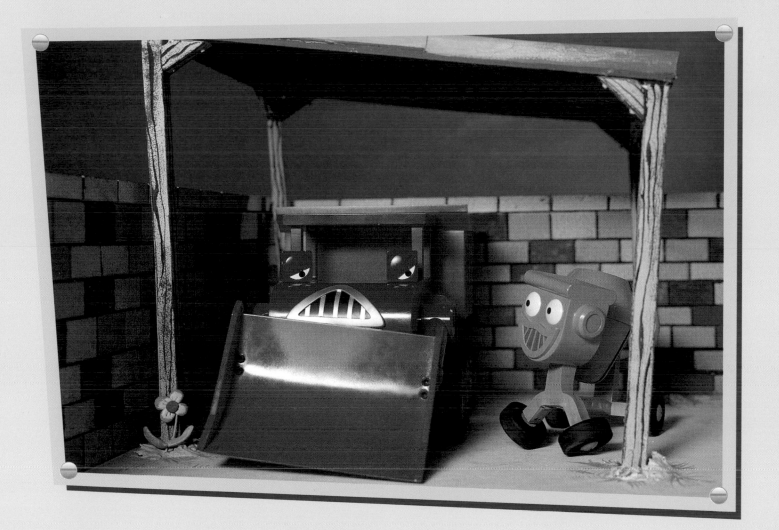

Later that night, just as the machines were drifting off to sleep, Dizzy nudged Muck.

"Muck," she whispered.

"Um…?" mumbled Muck.

"Wasn't I good at football today?" asked Dizzy.

Muck opened his mouth to reply, but something started tickling the back of his nose.

"**A-a-a-a-a-at-chhoo!**"
he sneezed.

"Now Muck's got
Bob's cold!"
chuckled Scoop.

"**A-ª-ª-ª-t-choo!**" sneezed Muck. "I'm not sure you were good, Dizzy, but you certainly got stuck in!"

THE END!

Scoop Has Some Fun

"We've got lots to do today," said Wendy. "Bob, you'd better be off! You've got those telegraph poles to put up. We'll be here stocktaking."

"What's stocktaking?" asked Roley.

"It's when you count up all of your equipment and make a list of what you have," Wendy explained. "You can make a start counting things in the yard, Roley."

"See you all later," said Bob as he hopped onto Scoop's step and left the yard.

"I'll count the pipes," Roley called. "One... two... three... four... err, what comes next?"

"Five!" said Dizzy.

Meanwhile, Wendy was in the office, "Let's see, seven pencils, four rolls of sticky tape, and what's this?" she said as she pulled out a bag from under the desk. "Oh, just Bob's old clothes. I don't think they need to go on the list!" she laughed.

Scoop finished digging a long row of holes for the telegraph poles while Bob rang Wendy.

"Hi, Wendy, I just called to say I'll be needing Muck and Lofty pretty soon," he said. "You've found some of my old clothes? I was going to take them to the recycling bin, but I forgot. OK then. Bye!"

"Well done, time for a break! I'll be back soon," he called to Scoop.

As soon as Bob had gone Spud popped up from behind a hedge.

"Hee, hee! What are you doing, Scoop?" he asked.

"Just having a break before I start work again," Scoop replied.

"You're always working," said Spud. "Why don't we have some fun?"

Scoop wasn't sure.

"What sort of fun?" he asked.

"You know... playing jokes!" said Spud.

"Well, it is my break," Scoop chuckled. And they set off in search of someone to play a joke on.

Scoop hid behind a haystack and left his front scoop poking
out. Spud put a bale of hay in the scoop and jumped on top.
Soon Travis came up the road.

"Do you like my magic bale of hay?" shouted Spud. "I can
make it fly."

"No, you can't," Travis replied.

"Watch this, then. **Abracadabra!**"
said Spud, then he whispered to Scoop,
"Lift me up now!"

Travis couldn't see Scoop at all, just Spud
on the bale of hay, floating in the air.

"Ooh, err! It's magic!" he yelled as he
whizzed off down the lane.

"Hee, hee, hee!" giggled Spud.

Next, Spud and Scoop went to Farmer Pickles's barn.
"Lift me up onto the roof and then go and hide,"
Spud ordered Scoop. "Hee, hee! Here comes Muck.
Just wait until he hears my voice in the sky," he chuckled.
"**Woooaahhh!**" he called loudly.

"Ohh, what's that?" asked Muck, skidding to a halt.
"Sounds like a ghost. I'm off!" he cried.

"Ha, ha! Now, let's go and find Lofty," Spud called
down to Scoop.

"I've got to get back to work," said Scoop.

"I'll find Lofty myself then," Spud said, crossly.

Lofty was on his way to Farmer Pickles's farm when suddenly Spud jumped out from behind a bush.

"**Boo!**" he shouted.

"**Waaghh!**" cried Lofty as he lost control and crashed into a pile of telegraph poles.

A pole got caught under his wheels and he tipped over.

"Help! I'm stuck!" he cried.

Spud looked worried. "I think I'd better go and get Bob!" he said.

"You've got to help. It's Lofty, he's stuck!"
panted Spud when he saw Bob further
down the lane.

"This had better not be another one of
your tricks," Scoop warned Spud.

"Honestly! You have to come!"
pleaded Spud.

"OK, let's go!" said Bob.

"Don't worry. We'll soon have you right side up!"
said Bob, when he saw Lofty.

"Right then, all together now!" Bob shouted as
he, Spud and Scoop all heaved together. Lofty tilted
slowly over and landed back on his wheels.

"Errr... thanks, Bob," Lofty stammered.

"Thank Spud, he was the one that came
for help," said Bob.

Spud looked worried, "Weeell, errr, it
was my fault really, Bob. I gave Lofty
a fright and that's how he got stuck!"

"Oh, Spud! Well, what do you say?"
asked Bob.

"Sorry, Lofty," muttered Spud.

The team got back to putting up the telegraph poles.

"That's another job well done, even if Spud's little pranks held us up," said Bob. "Hmm... I've got a great idea. I'll just ring Wendy."

Wendy had just finished stocktaking when her mobile rang.

"Oh hello, Bob. Yes, your clothes are still here. Do you want them? OK," she said.

Spud went back to his field to scare some crows. But when he got there, a new scarecrow was in his place!

"What's going on?" he cried.

"Didn't Farmer Pickles tell you? You're too naughty. He's asked me to do your job," the new scarecrow said.

"B... but what about me?" asked Spud.

Then the new scarecrow made a face.

"**Bleurrggh!**" he shouted.

"**Waahhh!**" Spud cried, jumping back. The new scarecrow took off his hat and pulled the straw away.

"Surprise, surprise, Spud," he said.

"Awww, it's you, Bob," cried Spud. "That's not funny!"

"Come on, Spud! I thought you liked a good joke," said Bob, and everybody laughed.

THE END!